QUANTUM PRAYERS

CITY MISSIONS CHURCH
SINGAPORE 2009

DAVID & BECKY VAN KOEVERING

ELSEWHEN RESEARCH, INC.
PO Box 4783
Cleveland, TN 37320
USA

Elsewhen

Copyright © 2010 by David Van Koevering
Published by Elsewhen Research, Inc.
2nd Printing 2011

ISBN: 978-1-4507-1998-8

Printer:

Wilson Ng
Akitiara Corporation Sdn. Bhd.
Malaysia
ii

To schedule a speaking event, contact:

David Van Koevering
PO Box 4783
Cleveland, TN 37320
USA
elsewhen@hotmail.com
www.davidvankoevering.com

These prayers have been taken from the Singapore Conference in 2009 at City Missions Church. They have been edited from the literal transcription of prayers for persons in attendance at the conference.

The cover design and all the artwork on Elsewhen products, including the www.davidvankoevering.com website is from the creative spirit of Cathy Arkle (www.cathyarkle.com) of The Thumbprint Group (www.thumbprintgroup.com) info@thumbprintgroup.com

MEDICAL DISCLAIMER

The information provided in this text is for informational purposes only. It is not to be construed as medical care or medical advice and is not a replacement for medical care given by physicians or trained medical personnel. *Elsewhen* does not directly or indirectly practice medicine, nor does it dispense medical advice, diagnosis, treatment or any other medical service. Always seek the advice of your physician or other qualified healthcare provider(s) when experiencing symptoms or health problems, or before starting any new treatment. *Elsewhen* is not to be held responsible for any inaccuracies, omissions, or editorial errors, or for any consequences resulting from the information provided. By continuing to read this book, readers indicate acceptance of these terms. Readers who do not accept these terms should not read the pages of this book, transcribed from a conference.

It is your responsibility to evaluate the information and results from tools we provide. If you are a health care professional, you should exercise your professional judgment in evaluating any information, and we encourage you to confirm the information contained in this book with other sources before undertaking any treatment or action based on it. If you are a consumer, you should evaluate the information together with your physician or another qualified health care professional.

Contents

Examples of Prayer

It is important to understand that even though we are offering these prayers as example to learn from and follow, you are to allow the Holy Spirit to lead you. Do not just pray these prayers as rote prayers. Let the Holy Spirit guide you as you pray for each person.

The Frequency of Intercession

The frequency of intercession is when you turn yourself off and let the full authority of God flow through you. We bring our limits, our ego, our confidence, and our lack of confidence to our prayers. Just turn yourself off and let the flow of God happen by saying...

- *Holy Spirit, rise strong within me.*
- *Rise strong in _____ (the name of the person you are praying for).*

Becky's Prayer for a Blood Shield

- *The Lord bless you.*

- *I pray a blood shield over all of you in Jesus' name, and over your families for protection with angelic protection over all of us and our loved ones and that our unsaved loves one will be saved, in Jesus' name. Amen.*

General Prayer 1

- *Father God, my sister came in faith believing in Your name and in the blood of Jesus. We know you are working in people's lives.*
- *We call forth my sister's healing, in Jesus' name.*
- *We call forth her miracle.*
- *Restore the right frequencies, Father.*
- *Give her the frequencies of health.*
- *Give her the frequencies of wellness.*
- *May her body remember these 31 pitches that the body needs, in Jesus' name.*
- *Cells in this body, obey the design of God. Obey the desire she has to serve you.*
- *We call her healed by the blood of Jesus Christ.*
- *We call her delivered. We call her set free.*
- *We call forth high levels of energy.*
- *All symptoms removed! Disease dismissed!*
- *We call her assignment being completed in her life.*
- *May she walk in wellness and health and may these frequencies remain in her body in Jesus' name.*
- *Give her energy, Lord, in Jesus' name.*

- *In the name of Jesus, may she walk in health, walk in wellness, walk with a vision of God flowing through her spirit, in Jesus' name.*

General Prayer 2

I am using a frequency plasma and healing music, so if you move your fingers while touching the plasma, you will see you are hooked up to the frequencies as you see them follow your fingers. As the frequencies of the music and my prayer enter your body, your internal frequencies will be raised to God's original design.

- *Father God I speak into my brother's body.*

- *I speak into his spirit and soul and say, "Jesus is healing this body and this spirit."*

- *Father God, I pray in Jesus' name that the right frequencies and the virtue of your blood flow through this body.*

- *Set him free of any sickness and disease.*

- *Give him his body's health and wellness.*

- *Your plan for his life, reveal it, release it in Jesus' name.*

- *Body, you are healed.*

- *You walk in health and energy, in Jesus' name.*

General Prayer 3

- *Father God, as my brother stands here and touches this plasma, may he be aware that energy is flowing into his body, energy from my voice, energy from the name of Jesus, energy from the blood of Jesus, even energy from these frequencies.*

- *May his body be healed.*

- *May he walk in wellness.*

- *May he stand in perfect health in the name of Jesus.*

- *We call him healed.*

- *We call him delivered.*

- *We call him well.*

- *Father give him the evidence of that wellness.*

- *Symptoms, decrease and be removed.*

General Prayer 4

Hear me speak. Just agree with these words. Deuteronomy 32:30 tells me that one can put 1,000 to flight, and two can put 10,000 to flight. So I put 1,000 to flight. My brother on the front row agrees with me and we put 10,000 to flight. My sister sitting next to him stands in unity and the three of us put 100,000 to flight. The next person agrees and we have 1,000,000. The person sitting next to her joins in agreement and we have 10,000,000, then the next person and 100,000,000 then 1,000,000,000 (one billion). One more person joins and we have 10,000,000,000 (ten billion), and we haven't even left the front row yet. I'm talking about the authority that comes from unity.

Put your hands on the plasma screen.

- *I speak into your body – wellness.*

If someone would touch the back of her body, you would feel this energy just coming right off her. Real light touch. You will feel that energy.

- *Father God, we pray in Jesus' name that this body is healed.*

- *We call into her body the energy from the blood, the energy from the broken body of Jesus, the energy from His sacrifice for our healing.*

- *May these frequencies restore her cells with the authority of your blood and the authority of your healing power, not my words, but your authority called into her body.*

- *Restore her body.*

7

- *Symptoms, you're gone. Wellness, you're there.*

- *May my sister's consciousness of the wellness of God change her life.*

You have a consciousness that God has healed you. He has delivered you. You will notice a difference in your life. You will wait different.

- *Thank you Father. Make her assignment clear.*

- *Fill her with her assignment in Jesus' name.*

- *We thank you for healing her Father.*

Can you feel the energy?

- *As my sister prays for others, may your healing virtue flow.*

You have authority in Jesus' name to call forth healing. Go there in Jesus' name. We have the authority of Jesus' name. When you call forth your healing, you will go back to this moment by memory because you are hooked up to this moment and cannot be disconnected, in Jesus' name. Hallelujah.

General Prayer 5

- *Father in Jesus' name we claim that my sister is healed.*

- *We claim she is delivered in Jesus' name.*

- *Cells, obey.*

- *DNA, come to the original design.*

- *May her body remember these frequencies and my words spoken with them into her body.*

- *Deliver her.*

- *Give her, Father, her gift of causing healing in Jesus' name, of family and friends and loved one, in Jesus' name.*

Now don't be afraid to pray for those around you who are sick. I know you believe in prayer and you have probably been praying, but you will have a new level, a new confidence. These words are in your body.

- *Thank you, Father, for the manifestation of your healing, in Jesus' name.*

General Prayer 6

Just absorb that energy. I've had people tell me that six and eight people deep, they could sense energy coming from the plasma. So if you want to just lay hands on his back or his shoulder, and connect two or three deep.

- *Father God, in Jesus' name, I thank you for this night.*
- *I thank you for his faith.*
- *I thank you for the confidence of these people.*
- *Reward them, Father, by healing them and setting them free.*
- *Body, be healed in Jesus' name.*
- *Be sustained. May the healing last.*
- *Symptoms, you are dismissed.*
- *May the virtue of healing stay with him.*
- *May he be able to pass that healing, as we all can, to those around us.*
- *Thank you, Father, for healing my brother.*
- *Give him that deep confidence.*

General Prayer 7

- *Father, I speak into my sister the healing virtue of Jesus, what He did on the cross, what He did with His broken body.*

- *May that healing virtue flow, in His name.*

- *We call forth her healing scripturally.*

- *Father, correct the vibrations in her body.*

- *May these frequencies go through her body and may they be remembered in her body.*

- *May order come from disorder.*

- *May healing come from sickness.*

- *Symptoms, you are dismissed.*

- *Body, remember this healing moment and these frequencies in Jesus' name.*

General Prayer 8

- *Father God, come upon my brother.*

- *May he sense Your presence, which he already does. May he sense Your presence, Your consciousness, Your healing virtue.*

- *May these sounds and my voice call forth his healing in the name of Jesus.*

- *We call forth the broken body, we call forth the promises that by your stripes, he is healed.*

- *I call him healed in Jesus' name.*

- *I call him a miracle in the name of Jesus.*

- *May these frequencies go in and stay in the memory of his body. Even the matter of this watch will hold these frequencies.*

- *Father, deliver him, heal him - even things he didn't know were wrong.*

- *Heal his body. Rebuild his body. Give him health and energy.*

- *May his assignment burn within him.*

- *May he find all the energy necessary to fulfill his assignment, in Jesus' name.*

General Prayer 9

God bless you, my sister. Move your fingers so you know you are hooked up to the plasma. Do you see the frequencies following your finger as they flow into your body?

- *We ask the blessing upon that flow.*

- *May healing virtues come from the virtue of Jesus, the healing blood, His broken body.*

- *By His stripes we are healed, calling forth the elders, laying on of hands. Father, we claim that in my sister's behalf.*

- *Heal her.*

- *Set her free of any affliction, any limited frequencies.*

- *We call her body whole.*

- *We call her body pure.*

- *We call her cells obedient.*

- *We call the DNA perfect, to its original design.*

- *May she use these ideas and concepts in turn as she prays for others, and may the gift of healing flow through her, even to others.*

- *Father give her evidence now, within the hour that there has been a change, and we thank you for it in Jesus' name.*

General Prayer 10

- *Father God, you know what he said and what he needs.*
- *Father, remove those problems.*
- *In the name of Jesus heal him.*
- *May virtue flow from your blood to his body.*
- *May he know his body is being healed by Jesus.*
- *Jesus would use vibrations. Jesus will use my voice.*
- *We call him healed in the name of Jesus.*
- *May his body remember these frequencies.*
- *May this energy remain in his body. May he know it is in his body.*
- *May everything he has asked for be done.*
- *We thank you Father for healing him and sustaining his healing.*

I think all healings can be sustained. I've had a new heart for several years now, and my heart is better today than it has ever been.

- Your body will have that level of healing in Jesus' name. I speak that into you in the name of Jesus.

Thank you Jesus.

General Prayer 11

- *Thank you Jesus. Thank you, Jesus, for healing my brother.*
- *I call his body whole in the name of Jesus.*
- *I call forth his wellness.*
- *Any disability or any disabled affliction, I dismiss it in Jesus' name.*
- *May the words go forth these frequencies into his body.*
- *May the frequencies of this body restore his body in Jesus' name.*
- *Cells obey.*
- *DNA come to the original design.*
- *Deliver him for his purpose for his assignment in Jesus' name.*
- *Disobedient cells, obey the design of God.*

Thank you Father.

General Prayer 12

- *Father God, I pray in Jesus' name for my sister's body to be made whole.*

- *I call her healed.*

- *I call her delivered.*

- *I call missing vibrations to be made whole.*

- *I pray my words, the words of Jesus — "you are healed" in Jesus' name.*

- *We call forth life.*

- *We dismiss sickness.*

- *We dismiss symptoms.*

- *We call forth a body with obedient cells.*

- *We call forth a calling and an assignment that's clear.*

- *We call forth the energy to walk in faith and even deliver faith to others.*

General Prayer 13

Put your hands right on the plasma. If you move your hands, you will see you are hooked up. If you move your fingers you will see the frequencies following them. Now (others) put your hands right on top of her hands.

- *I thank you right now for my sister's healing.*

- *I call her cells to obedience.*

- *I call her body whole.*

- *I call forth her wellness.*

- *I call forth her strength.*

- *There is no weakness. There is no sickness. There is no ailing. There are no symptoms in Jesus' name.*

- *We call her body restored. We call her spirit encouraged. We call forth her faith enlarged.*

- *May her body remember my words and the words that Jesus loves her and heals her by his blood. That's the virtue in Jesus' name.*

- *May these frequency signals from the plasma remain in her body to bring forth those 31 frequencies we know this body needs.*

- *We call her body well and healed in Jesus' name.*

Walk in wellness. Walk in healing, and when you find one that needs healing, share it.

General Prayer 14

- *Thank you Father for my sister. You know what she needs and you are giving that to her now.*

- *Healing virtue, flow through my sister.*

- *May she feel the energy of God moving through her body, through her cells in Jesus' name.*

- *Heal this body.*

- *Deliver this body in the name of Jesus.*

- *We thank you, Jesus, that you shed your life's blood; your body was broken for her healing so we claim that healing right now in the name of Jesus.*

- *All evil is dismissed.*

- *All blessings are released in Jesus' name.*

- *Go in health. Go in wellness.*

- *Go with your body remembering the healing of God in Jesus' name. God bless you.*

General Prayer 15

God is going to heal you. He is going to change you. You're going to find deliverance in Jesus' name.

- *Father God, in Jesus' name, I pray for my sister.*
- *I ask for her deliverance.*
- *I ask you for healing.*

She came with questions of healing, and Father God you have answered her with a confidence of being healed. When the church agrees, says yes she is healed, and she believes that, she admits that, and she says it, then she sees her healing.

- *I declare you are healed.*
- *The symptoms are gone.*

You will notice a change. You will rest tonight like you have not rested for weeks. When you awake, you will awake refreshed, and there will be no symptoms, in Jesus' name.

- *Father God, touch my sister.*
- *Satan, stop messing with her! You're dismissed. You're discharged. You have no rights here. You are an imposter here.*
- *No disease can hide in this body.*
- *We call her healed in Jesus' name.*
- *You are blessed. Thank you Lord for healing my sister. Amen.*

General Prayer 16

- *Father God, you know my brother's body. You know his system. You know him intimately, Lord. You're causing his body to be. If you didn't cause his body to be, his body would be dissolved so we ask you to heal him.*

- *We ask you to give him energy, to give him strength, to give him healing. Take care of this body, Father God.*

- *We pray that you come upon him now and cause healing from the top of his head to the bottom of his feet.*

- *Deliver him and set him free.*

- *We thank you, Father, for the restored faith he has.*

- *We thank you, Father, for the courage he has.*

- *We thank you for the prayers of the saints who are agreeing that our brother is healed in the name of Jesus.*

- *Thank you, Lord. We claim his healing in Jesus' name.*

God bless you my brother.

General Prayer 17

God knows all about all of you. He has already examined you. He knows perfectly well what is right and wrong in your body.

- *In His Son's name and by the authority of His blood, I ask that your body be healed. Father God, heal my brother.*

- *May he sense a virtue flowing from the top of his head down through his limbs and his organs, through his muscles, through his tendons, through the nerves and through the DNA.*

- *We call the DNA to the original design.*

- *Father, we observe the cells being obedient. They cannot be disobedient.*

- *Father, guide him to his assignment.*

- *Give him the strength and energy to have new energy every day, abundant energy and no lack of energy.*

- *Heal him and make him, Father, a witness of his healing.*

- *Speak to his doctor. Speak to his family telling his story.*

- *Speak through his life that he is healed and he has been delivered in Jesus' name.*

General Prayer 18

- *I call him made whole. I call his body touched.*
- *I call him healed.*
- *I call him delivered.*
- *I call him changed by the authority of the blood of Jesus Christ.*
- *Father God, touch him. May your virtue flow through his body, through his spirit, through his soul.*
- *Restore his joy and his wisdom and knowledge of knowing he has been rebuilt and redeemed by the blood of Jesus Christ.*
- *Heal him.*
- *Set him free.*
- *Set him on his assignment. May using his energy for the kingdom of God burn deeply within him.*
- *Walk in health.*
- *Nothing broken, nothing missing, nothing bent.*
- *Healthy and bright for Jesus Christ.*
- *Thank you for this Father.*
- *We declare him healed.*
- *Satan, stop messing with him.*
- *He is delivered and he is healed in Jesus' name.*

General Prayer 19

- *Father God, you know what's wrong with my sister.*

- *She could tell me what's wrong, but that wouldn't be important to know because I am speaking to her body from the top of her head down through her spirit through her body all the way to her feet.*

- *You are healing her body. You're fixing it.*

- *You're changing the cells that are wrong to cells that are correct and obedient.*

- *You're changing the DNA, Lord.*

- *Even the blood can be corrected, the nervous system, the organs, mostly the spirit.*

- *Father if we are walking close to you, our spirits merge with your Spirit, and your presence becomes who we are. We are living in your life and in your presence.*

- *You inhabit our praise. You inhabit our music. You inhabit our bodies.*

- *I speak virtue into every cell in my sister's body.*

- *What's wrong, we call it corrected.*

- *Anything missing, we call it restored.*

- *Anything of sickness or the memory of sickness, symptoms, we call it dismissed in Jesus' name.*

And you said... I am healed in Jesus' name.

General Prayer 20

God knows what's wrong with all of these bodies. He has already diagnosed you. He did that before you came here because in His spirit, the Spirit of God looking forward, He knew you would be here tonight. He knew. You will never get to a place where He has not been.

- *So we call you healed.*
- *We call you delivered.*
- *May you walk in the energy of youth and in perfect health with no sickness, no disease, and no limitations.*
- *By the name of Jesus, I call you delivered and thank you Father for restoring an old relationship, an old connection. Thank you for that, Father.*
- *May she walk in joy, walk in peace, and walk in health.*

God bless you my sister.

General Prayer 21

You need health and you need wellness. You need a healthy body. I'm going to call this body to its original design. God did not design it to be with disease or limits or ailments or pain.

- *Father God, in Jesus' name, I declare this body healed. The blood of Jesus Christ, the broken body and its purpose flows, that virtue for my sister. We call her body healed.*
- *We call her body delivered.*
- *Her body can have no more symptoms.*
- *We dismiss the symptoms and call her healed in Jesus' name.*

Some may ask, "How are you so sure that everyone is going to get healed?"

My God is no respecter of persons. He doesn't pick out the tough cases and overlook the easier ones. He doesn't just heal the easy ones and overlook the tough ones. He's going to heal you like He healed me. If your desire is to have a body that's healthy for His assignment, I guarantee that He heals you. That is what He did to me. I couldn't leave this planet. My assignment wasn't done.

- *Your assignment. I call it forth. May her assignment be so clear that she can write it down in Jesus' name.*
- *I speak to her body, I speak to her jaw, I speak to her nerves, I speak to her tissues,*

*I speak to anything that has had a symptom.
I call it corrected in Jesus' name.*

Now you have to thank God for your healing, and
when you feel a pain you have to dismiss that pain in
Jesus' name. I'm not telling you to overlook it and
deny it. I'm telling you to dismiss it. It has to leave.

- *Satan, you can't lie to my sister.*

- *You're dismissed, Satan, and your lies go with
  you.*

- *She walks in health, in Jesus' name.*

God bless you and rejoice.

General Prayer 22

- *Father God, we pray that you would touch this brother's spirit. Touch him, Father, in body mind and spirit.*

- *I call forth his assignment that would be the desire of his life, to do the bidding and will of God, to be a kingdom builder.*

- *He needs a neck that doesn't hurt, so Father God, remove the tensions.*

- *Remove the difficulties.*

- *Work through his body and set him free.*

- *Change him, Father, into the kingdom builder you designed him to be.*

- *We see past sickness, we see past difficulties, we see past limits and call him healed and delivered. He knows Father, you're a God of healing. You've done it before.*

- *I call him healed from the top of his head to the bottom of his feet.*

- *In Jesus' name fill him with your wisdom to do your will in Jesus' name.*

General Prayer 23

- *Father God, you heard my sister. You know her heart and her intent.*

- *I ask your healing virtue to flow, even from the top of her head down through her body.*

- *May the energy of God heal this body.*

- *Heal the mind.*

- *Heal the body, every cell, every DNA.*

- *Go through the body. Wherever there is a weakness, we call it strong.*

- *Wherever there has been sickness or disease, we call it healed.*

- *You walk in perfect health to do your assignment and your purpose in Jesus' name.*

Say with me...

- *I am healed completely, in my spirit, in my mind, and in my body in Jesus' name.*

- *Thank you, Jesus, for healing me.*

General Prayer 24

Father God, you know where my sister is. You know her heart. You know why she stood in line. You know what she has just uttered. You know her, Father. You are reading her mail[1]. You know her intent.

- *We call her healed.*
- *We call forth deliverance.*
- *We call forth the answer to the intent of her heart, the intent of other hearts that have been intending.*
- *We called her intent complete.*
- *Bless her. May she know your presence and know her authority and know her assignment, in Jesus' name.*
- *May your virtue flow through her right now.*
- *May she sense your presence.*
- *May she know that it's on the inside moving through her and reaching out through her intent to others, in Jesus' name.*
- *Give her that healing.*
- *Give her that new authority.*

Say after me, "I thank you Lord for my new authority, in Jesus' name. Amen and Amen."

---

[1] "Reading your mail" means the Lord knows what you are thinking.

General Prayer 25

How do you want me to pray for you? So I'm going to pray that you are just healed. Is that okay?

- *Father God, you know this young man, you know his heart.*

- *You know what he thinks is wrong.*

- *Father, we ask that you would give him a revelation that he has been healed and that he has been delivered.*

- *Give him that consciousness.*

- *So we call him healed.*

- *Whatever the ailment, whatever the elements are, whatever the pieces are, I call him healed in the name of Jesus, and delivered by the authority of the name of Jesus Christ.*

Amen and Amen.

General Prayer 26

- *You have been believing for healing for some time. We call it done right now.*

- *We call her body healed in the name of Jesus. The virtue of your blood, the blood of Jesus, blessed by the Father, called forth by his design.*

- *Her body walks in health. She walks in healing.*

- *Cells are obedient.*

- *All wrong is dismissed.*

- *All symptoms are gone.*

- *Her body remembers these frequencies and this prayer.*

- *Father God, as she finds those loved ones, those friends, may she be able to share her healing.*

Prayer by an 8-Year-Old Boy

A few months ago a minister called an eight-year-old boy out of the audience and asked him to pray for a man with a broken neck and two tungsten rods in his neck. The boy said...

- *Body, you are healed in Jesus' name.*

An eight-year-old boy had enough evidence and confidence to say...

- *God, you are going to heal my friend...*

...and God healed his friend. I was there. I saw it happen. They took x-rays afterward and the rods were gone. We are going to publish those X-rays on our website, the X-rays with the rods and without the rods.

Prayer for Assignment 1

God has a major assignment for you. I don't know what it is but you may know.

- *Whatever help you need for your assignment, I'm going to declare that to flow into your body.*

- *So I say to you in Jesus' name, you are healed.*

- *You are set free.*

- *Emotional difficulties, spiritual difficulties, physical difficulties are removed, and you walk in life.*

- *You walk in health. No sickness here. No disease here. No missing or ailing energies here.*

- *Father God, give him the energy and the strength for his assignment in Jesus' name.*

Prayer for Assignment 2

You have to be conscious and wanting your assignment because He will meet all the needs for your assignment. Now that's the message I have. Someone else has a different way of stating it. That could very well be, but...

- *I pray for this man's assignment, that you know why you're here, and tomorrow know your purpose.*

- *You will have all the energy you need, and all the help you need.*

- No pain in the neck or anyplace else.

Resources for this assignment are yours too.

34

Prayer for Autism

- *Thank you, Father, for healing my brother.*
- *Thank you, Father, for making him whole.*
- *May those who know and love him, know there is a change going on right now.*
- *Give symptomatic changes.*
- *Give refraction changes.*
- *Father, come upon my brother and deliver him of any weakness, any limit.*
- *He is healed by Jesus in Jesus' name. Thank you, Father.*

You will see a difference in Jesus' name. Thank you my brother. God bless you. Thank you.

Prayer for Body and Spirit

I'm going to pray for your body and your spirit.

- *Father God, you know my sister.*

- *We declare that she is healed, that she has been set free, even as this music is playing in the background. It is being recorded and my voice is getting recorded in the cross.*

- *So Father God give her the comfort to know that the memory of this time is in that cross, and that Your presence is always there, and that she can ask for the play back of your peace in your presence, and 10 times out of 10, You will play it back.*

- *Father, give her that experience. May she know she is healed.*

- *Any sickness, any difficulty, we call it dismissed.*

- *May she not dwell on it, but may she claim that she is delivered.*

- *May she walk in health for her assignment.*

- *Make the assignment clear.*

- *Show her how to build your kingdom, and share this healing moment with others, in Jesus' name.*

Often our healing is not only for ourselves. Mine wasn't just for me. As dramatic as a brand-new heart is, it wasn't for me only. Now I know how to call that forth, and your healing will give you that authority.

So say with me...

- *Jesus, I'm glad I'm healed.*
- *I am a healer.*
- *I can speak healing into others in Jesus' name.*
- *Thank you for healing me.*
- *Thank you for healing them.*

And you will find them. You will find them in front of you and simply declare their healing. You don't have to remember everything I say. He will remind you of enough to get the job done. Thank you, Jesus. Hallelujah.

Prayer for a Building

There is an important conference coming to town. We collectively aim ourselves over toward the Sun Tent Center. We put our focused energy on that big building with the big TV screen in front of it. Right now we declare:

- *That building is a place for righteousness.*

They're going to be talking about your financial future in that building. You have the opportunity to change that place with your prayer, your intent.

So we focus our attention on that building. I just look at it out the window, and you agree with me. I declare:

- *We call forth righteousness.*

- *May Obama and the others who are coming from all over the world have righteousness surfacing in their consciousness.*

You see, the Holy Spirit will guide your leadership. **God ideas only come from the Holy Spirit.**

God ideas are needed in our economy now more than ever. There is more to fix than to build. We have a lot of mistakes that still aren't fixed. Oh, they might not talk about it a lot, but they are trying to find solutions.

- *I declare the solution is righteousness, salvation and deliverance.*

Prayer for Business

God is the God of business, too.

- *In your business partners, I pray that you would have unity and good communication.*

- *You will stand in unity and not be indifferent.*

- *Father God, we pray for the resources of business, for the success of business.*

- *Confusion dismissed.*

- *We call forth peace, the presence of God, the blessings of God, the success of God, the resources of God.*

- *Bless the business.*

- *May it expand and grow.*

- *Difficulties dismissed, in Jesus' name.*

As you work in the business, during the day you can commit ideas to God, and if you don't have an answer, say...

- *Lord, give me the answer.*

He will guide you and bless you. Thank you Jesus. God bless you.

Prayer for a Brother

Put your hands this way. We're going to pray for a brother.

- *As I speak to my sister, I call forth her brother's deliverance.*

- *Demonic activity dismissed. Dismissed!*

- *Alter him right now.*

Remember, we are "x (times) 10," so there is a large force leaving us right now going out to a brother. My authority x 10 x 10 x 10 x 10. We direct that to your brother. You are going to say his name, and we call him delivered.

- *We call him delivered. He is delivered.*

- *Depression leave.*

- *Obsessions leave.*

- *Deliver him in Jesus' name, and may this sister get word tonight from him, tonight Lord, that he has been delivered. May he call, may there be evidence, may there be an instance where she knows tonight, Lord.*

We can be specific in our requests. We call him forth delivered tonight, in Jesus' name. Say, "Tonight," Church. This isn't going to happen over a week. It is going to happen now. This person is delivered in Jesus' name. Thank you for bringing your brother to our attention. We're connected to him through you. Thank you, Father. God bless you.

Prayer for a Child's Salvation

Father God, you know our heart for a child. We are your children, and you know our children.

- *Speak, Father, to this child.*
- *Deliver this child.*
- *Put people in his path to minister to this child.*
- *Give Mom the desire of her heart.*
- *May her intensity not fail.*
- *May her zeal and her persistence for salvation not change.*
- *May that child be delivered soon, even within days.*
- *We call deliverance, in Jesus' name. Amen and Amen.*

Prayer for a Couple

- *I call my brother and sister into perfect health.*
- *I call them into perfect finance.*
- *I call them into perfect peace.*
- *I call their relationship to each other and to every family member and to every business associate – healthy.*
- *Spirit guided relationships. Bless them.*
- *My sister's body - every cell is obedient. Every cell is becoming obedient to the voice of God.*
- *No sickness.*
- *No disease.*
- *My brother, the energy of your youth, the energy of your youth, we call it forth.*
- *May you walk in perfect health.*
- *Pain, you have no place here.*
- *Sickness, you have no place here. Thank you, Father, for healing.*
- *Thank you, Father, for total and complete deliverance.*
- *May they walk in the height of their calling.*
- *May they walk into the perfect righteousness you have for their ministry.*
- *The Lord knows these aren't business people; they are ministers. They are ambassadors of*

Jesus Christ and the building of His kingdom. Birth that in them every hour of every day.

- *Give them the wisdom to walk in their assignment.*

- *Fulfill the desires of their hearts. Their hearts are pure.*

You can have God desires. Your desire is the strongest thing you can have.

- *We call your desires pure. We call your desires fulfilled. The desire you have, the purpose you have, the intent you have, we call it complete.*

- *Bless this couple.*

- *Remove all limits. Remove all limits.*

- *Take them to the highest places.*

Prayer for a Son

You don't have to accept it. We're not denying it. It's there, but it can't stay there because you have Jesus' authority, which is greater than the authority of anything that's wrong. You've got it. What else?

- *Father God, you know what he has just said.*

- *You know about his son.*

- *You know about the healing and deliverance.*

- *The greatest gift his father can give is the confidence that he is complete in Jesus, completely healed, completely delivered, completely protected, completely enabled, completely prepared for his assignment.*

- *So, Father God, I pray that you would give this father that confidence.*

- *Bless him Father.*

- *That energy goes from here. We are connected to that son through the father, right here.*

- *So, Father, we call him altered; we call him healed.*

Prayer for a Son (Standing In)

My sister is standing in for Brian. Church, we're going to pray for Brian.

- *He's delivered.*
- *He is healed.*
- *Demonic activity is set free from Brian.*
- *Father God, you know this man. You made this man.*
- *Heal him in Jesus' name and set him free.*
- *Mom's desire is honored right now.*
- *Her body is healed.*
- *Her son is delivered and set free.*
- *Thank you, Jesus.*
- *He is healed. We see him healed.*
- *We see him normal.*
- *We see him playing. We see him running and rejoicing. We see him living for Jesus.*
- *His assignment is clear in his spirit, as it's clear in Mom.*

Prayer for a Son's Salvation

Father God, you know this mother's heart for her son's salvation. We couple with her x 10 x anyone else who's agreeing, Father, that he would be led to Jesus soon.

- *Change his circumstances.*
- *Change his plans and his appointments and his friends, his acquaintances.*
- *Put him on a trajectory to cross paths with people who will effectively minister to him, in Jesus' name. May that happen soon.*
- *Win Him, in Jesus' name.*
- *Give Mama the desire of her heart.*

I advise you to pray for his friends that some of them get changed. I felt as I could see him, I could see his friends. That's part of his problem. Call forth new friends. Call forth Christian friends.

- *Father, put Christians in his life.*
- *May he find acquaintances and find interests with those who are children of God.*
- *We rebuke the friends that are children of evil.*
- *Cause him to be delivered because of his friends, in Jesus' name.*
- *Thank you, Father. Amen.*

Prayer for Cancer

None of that medical report is news to God. He did not need the doctor to tell you so you could complain to him. He knows it already. He knows every instance of your future, and He has already been there to fix it. He knew you were going to be here.

He knew who was going to be here to pray with us, so we stand united. We stand in unity. We have Christians from many walks of life here, and God loves you. He's not through with you. You can't be sick unto anything that limits. He has a purpose for every day of your life.

- *Father God, I pray in Jesus' name for my sister's body to be touched right now.*

- *As real as she feels my hand on her hand, may she sense your hand and your virtue and the warmth of your healing flow through her body.*

- *You know where to go in the tissues.*

- *Father, you gave me a brand-new heart. It was full of disease, and now there is nothing wrong. Father God, you can touch this sister's heart and every cell in every part of every tissue in her body.*

- *So as the sound of this music is going through her body, and my voice is going through her mind and her body, I call forth healing through her body.*

- *She is healed in Jesus' name.*

- *She is delivered in Jesus' name.*

- *It's going to shock some doctors to find out that their former diagnosis was flawed, but in fact what they saw may have been there. But Father, You're removing that now.*

- *You're taking away fear.*

- *You're taking away concern.*

- *You're taking away negative thoughts.*

- *You're taking away all that Satan has lied to my sister about.*

- *Her life isn't over. She is not going to have to be cut on or radiated on in any way.*

- *She's going to walk in perfect health. As Jesus walked the shores of Galilee, He touched and He healed.*

- *I declare her healed by the authority of Jesus.*

- *As His ambassador, I say to this sister, you are healed.*

- *You are delivered. You are set free.*

- *So now we thank you, Father.*

- *It's like she has the check; now she has to cash it. The check is her promise. Her joy is when she cashes it, and she knows the joy of deliverance, the joy of healing, the joy of no fear in Your name.*

- *Satan, stop lying to my sister.*

- *You can't put fear in her. The presence of God is here.*

- *She is going to walk in health in Jesus' name.*

When I talk to someone who is sick, I remember what it was like when my heart would shut off. Becky and I did not deny that my heart was shutting off. We did not deny that I had a heart full of disease. We never denied it, not once. We never denied that I died. **I just *believed* for my new heart.**

I rejoiced and promised God that every day of my life was His. With that commitment made, I am His servant.

He will do what He promised because He loves you. You are his kid; He's your dad. Daddy doesn't lie to his daughter. He cannot lie to you. He is healing you.

- *Father, may that virtue flow even as she rests tonight.*
- *May she know that she is healed.*
- *May the doctors give her evidence that she is healed.*

When I pray for anyone with a disease, I tell you to go back to your doctor and get your evidence of healing because I know it's going to be there. It happened with me. It will happen for you with your eye pressure. Go there. We prayed for my brother's back.

Go back to your doctor with faith and with confidence. Let him prove that you've been healed. Don't go for a check up with doubt in your heart. You do not doubt.

- *We dismiss doubt in Jesus' name. Hallelujah.*

Prayer for Disability

I have a confidence that when I pray, whatever the sickness, it has to go. I don't believe sickness came to you by God's authority. I don't think it got here because he's trying to tell you something. I think sickness is from Satan who kills, steals and destroys. If I see things that cause death, pain, and destruction, I blame it on Satan. I know he's the author if it so I have no thought of God doing some good by making use of it. Yes, He can do things to make you better, but He can completely heal. That's what Jesus came to do. Jesus healed them all. He wasn't selective.

I'm not selective either, so whatever your problem is, God knows it and you know it. As you say to Jesus, heal me, and when you say what's wrong, he is going to hear your prayer.

- *Father God, in Jesus' name, I declare my little sister's healing.*

- *She walks with a new body.*

- *She walks with a healthy body.*

- *There is no limit, there is no pain, there is no suffering.*

- *There are no self-imposed limits here. The limits are removed physically.*

- *She walks in health. I claim her health.*

- *She is a witness and a testimony to the miracles of Jesus Christ.*

- *I thank you for her.*

- *Heal her.*

- *May she be in other services of this conference and testify that she has been healed.*

- *Pain and symptoms are gone in Jesus' name.*

Prayer for Disease

- *Father God, I speak into my sister's body. You know the deficiency.*
- *You know the wrong frequencies,*
- *You know the problems that we call forth to be corrected.*
- *We call her body healthy.*
- *We call her mind and her spirit to have faith in the name of Jesus, faith in the blood of Jesus.*
- *We call her healed and a miracle to happen in her life, in Jesus' name.*
- *We thank you, Father, for her healing.*
- *Body, remember these frequencies!*
- *Disease, you're dismissed.*
- *Lack of faith, you're dismissed.*
- *Fill my sister with the faith of Jesus, in Jesus' name.*

Now change will come. Change is something you can do in how you observe your body, how you observe your health in the name of Jesus. ***Change how you observe your body.***

Prayer for Disease (Chronic) 1

- *Father God, in the name of Jesus, we pray for our sister.*

- *You know her body. You're causing her body to be.*

- *Father, we call forth, in the name of Jesus, her healing, her deliverance, her health.*

- *May she have favor right now, in Jesus' name.*

- *May frequencies that her body needs go into her body.*

- *We call her healed.*

- *We call her delivered in the name of Jesus.*

Now sister, your body has memory.

Those who have had shattered bones from accidents and had to amputate an arm still feel the pain after the arm has been removed. I'm saying that to tell you your body has memory. Her body will remember these frequencies. Her body is taking in information right. **The body has memory.**

- *So I call forth that your body will remember these frequencies, and you can't be broken from it. The memory will stay there.*

Prayer for Disease (Chronic) 2

- *My sister, with the authority vested in me by use of His name, in Jesus' name, I declare that you are healed. This group is in unity, Father.*

- *We ask you in the name of Jesus to deliver my sister.*

- *Cells obey.*

- *Disease, you're dismissed.*

- *Disorder, you're dismissed. You cannot be here in her body.*

- *DNA, you are corrected.*

- *Disease is out of here.*

- *Fear is out of here.*

- *All the effect of Satan is dismissed.*

- *I bless you in Jesus' name.*

- *I declare you healed.*

- *This church agrees. That unity is expressed.*

Walk ye in health and give God thanks in Jesus' name, my precious sister. God knows all about it. He designed your body. Jesus is sustaining all things.

- *So I say, Father God in Jesus' name, deliver my sister.*

- *Muscles, become obedient. Muscles, you are healed.*

- *Organs in her body, you are healed.*

- *Tendons, you are healed.*

- *Bones, you are healed.*
- *Circulation you are healed.*
- *Nervous system, you are healed.*
- *Mind you are healed.*
- *Brain you are healed in the name of Jesus.*

I believe that it is possible for your body to remember pain, and I want to dismiss the memory of pain and the memory your body could have of symptoms.

...dismiss the memory of symptoms...

I told you about people who had organic heart transplants, and their whole life changed because their new heart remembered the old body. An arm can be removed that has been shattered in war, and the person will still feel pain the rest of their life because the body remembers pain.

- *I dismiss from you my sister the memory of pain so that when you are healed, your body cannot be disobedient and play games with you.*
- *You are healed.*
- *The pain is gone.*
- *The disorder is gone, and if you move your leg you will find that it is not the same as it was when you came in here.*
- *You are changed by the authority of Jesus Christ Who flows through your body.*

Prayer about Evil Spirits

He can go before you and make that path straight.

- *Father, go before my sister.*

- *Before she gets there, even the next time she enters, may she have the peace that you have already fixed the problem.*

- *So Father God, we come against the spirits of evil that are in that place.*

- *We dismiss them from her presence.*

- *We dismiss them from affecting her.*

- *Father God, send angelic forces to fight her battle.*

- *May you prepare her place even in the wilderness.*

- *Set her free there to witness carefully and to witness correctly and to work with the children.*

- *And Father, the evil spirits she is talking about... Demons, dismissed. You must leave.*

- *You cannot show up in my sister's presence. This is the glory of God. This is the presence of God. This is the authority of Jesus' name.*

- *You cannot enter her space or her place.*

And when you come into the building, you just say,

- *Jesus, your authority surrounds me. Angelic forces go before me...*

...and don't get upset with the people. That would be wrestling with flesh and blood. Paul said we are not to wrestle with flesh and blood. (Ephesians 6:12) Go directly to the principalities and say...

- *Satan, you're dismissed.*

When you walk through the door, let that be your prayer. You will find a whole new authority and a whole new peace. Satan cannot be where God's authority is. Say it with me...

- *Satan cannot be where God's presence is.*

And his presence is in you. When your presence manifests, Satan cannot mess with you. We have all put up with too much. So let's get rid of him. **Learn how to dismiss Satan and be done with it.**

You are a warrior, not with your words, but with your prayers. The prayer to dismiss is your authority.

So when you see a problem, you can even say it out loud. You don't care if they hear it. It doesn't matter, but don't get into an argument. If they try to get you in an argument, say, "I prefer not to argue." Just say,

- *Satan, you're dismissed.*

He has to leave, and they can't mess with you because they have to break your smile. Your smile is from Jesus. They can't get that. You are a warrior. Go win that war. That's an easy one.

Prayer for Eyes

You look good, but you don't see well. Your eyes are important. Your spiritual eyes are important, and your physical eyes are important. Your eyes control your imagination, your inner vision, as well as your physical vision. So when I pray for the eyes, I pray for the physical eyeball in the socket, for the physiological condition that causes sight to happen.

- *I say in Jesus' name that he is healed.*

- *The eyes are restored.*

- *The dimension of the eyeball is corrected.*

- *The conditions of the eyeball are corrected.*

- *Whatever is wrong with the compounds and the pieces in the eyes, the parts of the eyes, the entire eye nerves, the seeing part of the brain, we call it corrected in Jesus' name.*

- *As real as He created it in your mother's womb, He has the authority to correct it. Right now in the name of Jesus, I call his eyes healed.*

- *I call them changing.*

- *I call them being delivering.*

- *I pray that his eyes, and also his spiritual eyes, see what God wants him to see.*

- *Even though there is a physical thing we are praying for, the eyeball, I am impressed to pray for the spiritual eye of what you have to see in the kingdom.*

What you are going to see in the kingdom is your assignment, things you are to do. You are going to see them clearly and spiritually. You are going to see all the pieces of those visions, all the pieces of those plans, all the purposes he has for your life.

- *So physical eyes, we call you corrected in Jesus' name.*

- *All symptoms and disease dismissed.*

- *We call forth spiritual eyes and vision for his future.*

- *Make it so clear he cannot miss it.*

- *Father, let that virtue flow through his body. Let it flow through his organs, through his tendons, through his tissues, his circulation.*

- *Adrenaline, become obedient.*

- *Hormones, become obedient.*

- *Bones and muscles are corrected.*

- *He is healed in Jesus' name. Thank you, Father, for healing.*

- *Thank you, Father for giving him brand-new eyes.*

- *Father God, when he goes back to the eye doctors, may they declare a miracle has happened, that his eyes are different, like they did my heart. Nothing wrong, nothing broken, nothing missing.*

- *Give him that testimony for your glory Lord. He will share that testimony in Jesus' name. God bless you.*

Prayer for Finances 1

The difficulties are God's. Only fight the battle you can win. Some of these battles you can't win, so you surrender them to him and say Father, heal me. I don't have the money for an operation. I don't have the money to go to a clinic. You don't have to have the resources if you have the eternal resource. That resource is Jesus.

He is our Savior. His blood does the same for all of us. We are healed by His word that He gave us. You can ask anything in His name and it shall be done. (John 14:13)

- *So you're delivered.*
- *You're going to find resources.*
- *Miracles are released in your life.*
- *Funding and other needs are met in Jesus' name.*

All you have to do is be sincere when you are before the Father. ***Be grateful.***

You say, "Oh, I have to do more than that."

No, all you have to do is have a grateful heart because He will bring the money to you.

You say, "Well I have to go out and get clever tomorrow."

No you don't have to go out and get clever. Just be humble. Stay committed. Know your assignment and say it over and over.

What is your purpose? Most of you have kids and grandkids so you don't have to go very far to find part of that purpose. Your purpose includes your family, the people in the context of your environment, the domain that you have, the people you work with, the people you live with, the people who are around you.

You are a king with a domain. The domain is your contacts. Yours is different from mine.

- *We call forth that domain, filled with wisdom and the mind of God, in Jesus' name.*

Prayer for Finances 2

- *Father God, you know this brother. He is not broke and you're not broke.*

- *Guide him Father to your resources.*

- *Guide him to the sources that are his resources.*

- *Father, direct him.*

- *Bless him.*

- *Pour out abundance on him.*

- *Give him the spirit of good judgment.*

- *Give him the spirit of wisdom, in Jesus' name.*

Prayer for Frequencies

- *Frequencies, body's needs, we fill you in the name of Jesus.*

- *We call these frequencies to go into your body and heal your body and set your body free.*

- *You are delivered.*

- *It is the authority of the blood that is healing you and setting you free.*

- *Body, remember these frequencies.*

- *Prayer, you are going to be remembered in this body.*

- *Body, you are healed.*

- *Cells obey.*

- *DNA, come to the original design, in the name of Jesus.*

Prayer for Friend

We're going to pray for a friend.

- *Father God, you know this person she is standing in proxy for.*
- *So as I lay hands on her, I'm laying hands on him; as we are praying to her face, we are praying to his face.*
- *We are connected by her understanding of who he is.*
- *So Father, we call him saved.*
- *We call him delivered.*
- *We call forth God's purposes in his life.*
- *Sin, dismissed.*
- *Satan, dismissed.*
- *Friends and influence change.*
- *He is delivered in Jesus' name.*

Amen and Amen. Hallelujah. Thank you Jesus.

Prayer for Going to Higher Places

The book of Ephesians talks about higher places five times. I don't know if you mark in your Bible, but I do. I marked five places in the book of Ephesians on higher places. I recommend that you do the same, and then let the Holy Spirit guide you how to get to those higher places. You will find victory. You will find healing. You will find resources simply from the higher places.

- *Father, take them to higher places.*

- *Touch their mind with higher truth and better understanding.*

- *May they become the true teachers of the Word of God.*

- *May their house truly be a beacon, a light-house, a place of truth and refuge.*

- *They are blessed in Jesus' name.*

Prayer for Hands

Father God, you know the difficulty. You created this body. It is really your body Lord. My sister commits her life to you and her body to you. You are healing her hands. Father God, you're going to hear that prayer. You are going to give her that desire. We the believers, the group here in this church, are asking you to touch this body.

- *So Father, fix this body.*

You know what's wrong. Some doctors may know what's wrong. She may know what's wrong.

- *Father, we call the wrong "gone."*

- *We called the diseases dismissed.*

- *We call the cells to obedience.*

- *We call the DNA to its original design.*

- *Chemicals, obey.*

- *Bones, substances, tissue, organs obey.*

- *Obey the voice of God now that we speak into her saying "You are healed in Jesus' name."*

- *Thank you, Father. Thank you, Jesus for your healing.*

- *Show her assignment to her, why she's been healed.*

- *She's going to walk in health.*

- *Give her that assignment and heal this body.*

- I call it healed in Jesus' name.

Prayer for a Heart

This is a good place to be for a heart problem. I am real good at praying for hearts, because I know what God's done in my physical heart. He has done it for me, so then I speak to this heart.

- *All symptoms in his heart, and anything else in this body, any concerns about a heart problem, any fear that's been here in the spirit, Father God, I call it healed.*

- *I call him delivered.*

- *I call the heart to its original design, to the design of the designer.*

- *A new heart in Jesus' name.*

- *New arteries in Jesus' name.*

My arteries were so bad they put two 3½-inch stints in me, and now they can't find a thing wrong with the heart.

- *Father God, you did that for my heart. Do that for my brother's heart.*

- *May he know his assignment and live to fulfill it. With the energy of healing, may he fulfill his assignment.*

- *Touch the rest of his body, Lord.*

- *We call him healed.*

Prayer for House 1

I want both husband and wife to come for this prayer.
Let's bless your house.

- *I call your house a holy place.*
- *I call it delivered.*
- *I call it full of joy.*
- *I call it a place of God, the presence of God, with the sounds of prayer, the sounds of praise.*
- *Any evil that has ever been spoken in or around it is dismissed.*
- *Holy Spirit, move through that place. It is a holy place.*
- *It is a place of refuge.*
- *It is a place of healing.*
- *It is a place of deliverance.*
- *Now we can call the bodies of this husband and wife blessed.*
- *Father, I don't need to know what you already know because I don't know what to do about it except say healing and health and wellness flows in Jesus' name. We say it in Jesus' name because you told us, Jesus, that whatever we ask in Your name, believing, it would be done.*

Prayer for House 2

- *We call your house blessed.*
- *We call it delivered.*
- *No evil vibration comes through your house into this body from any source.*
- *We call your house blessed. Father, bless this house. You know the address.*
- *May angelic hosts, the Holy Spirit's authority, the virtue of Jesus Christ that was in the Passover blood be there.*
- *You are the Lamb that was slain, Lord. The virtue of that blood is on her doorpost.*
- *May she even anoint her doorpost with oil when she gets home. Make the oil in the shape of a cross on a spot.*

If I don't have oil, I use my own DNA. That's good anointing oil.

- *Call your house blessed.*
- *Call your car blessed.*
- *Call your finances blessed.*
- *Call your body blessed.*
- *Any limits and any ailments of the body are dismissed.*
- *I know it's not God's will for you to have pain or to have the difficulty that you are experiencing.*

- *So I call that difficulty dismissed in Jesus' name.*

- *She is healed in Jesus' name.*

- *She is delivered in Jesus' name.*

- *And Satan, no more messing with my sister.*

- *You're dismissed. You can't show up.*

- *You can't intimidate. You can't work through others.*

- *Your influence is dismissed from her life.*

- *Satan is dismissed.*

- *He has to leave her alone.*

- *He can't cause any problems.*

- *I speak to your mind and your memory, that your body will not remember symptoms because your symptoms are healed and delivered in Jesus' name.*

- *Father, may my sister see change quickly.*

- *May she testify of change. May she give witness of change, and where ever there has been a doctor involved, may he find the evidence of change.*

- *We call it done, healed.*

And my sister said, Thank you Jesus.

Prayer for House (Blessing)

You have authority to use Jesus' name correctly. Let me give you an example of using Jesus' name correctly. We're going to change your house. Say with me,

- *Father God, in Jesus' name I declare with my authority as the Bride of Christ that my house is blessed in Jesus' name.*

- *It's safe. Say it again, it's safe.*

- *No harm can happen here.*

- *Jesus' authority rules my house.*

- *Peace and glory fill my house.*

- *Praise and honor are the sounds of my house.*

- *My home is a welcome place.*

- *Jesus is there, and He is taught there, and lives are changed there, in Jesus' name.*

- *My house is full of peace.*

- *My house is full of health.*

- *Satan has no right there. I rebuke Satan from my house.*

- *Satan has no rights there. He is an imposter, and he is dismissed in Jesus' name.*

Whether you know it or not, you just altered your house. You just changed the value of your house. Your insurance premiums could come down, if the insurance company knew about this because it's a different place.

Prayer for an Intercessor 1

- *Father God, heal this body.*

- *May it be a perfect example of walking by faith.*

- *May there be no limits in this body.*

- *Restore her youth, Father.*

- *All aches and all pains and all difficulty, all soreness, and any symptoms, dismissed in Jesus' name!*

- *I speak into her nervous system and call it whole.*

- *I speak into your body and your organs and your skin and call them healed.*

- *Every cell is obedient. Every cell is rejoicing. Every cell is praising.*

- *She is praise. Praise isn't something you do. Praise is something you are.*

- *Thank you for her praise. As she praises, may miracles happen around her life.*

- *You will set the captives free.*

- *Father, make clear that list, that fresh list, that new list. May it happen daily when faces come to my sister.*

You will see them. You will remember them. You may even hear their voice, not a wrong voice, but through the Holy Spirit, the voice of the one you are to pray for. You are an intercessor, and that is your assignment. Intercession is not just what you do.

Intercession is the possession and acknowledgement of who you are. You are intercession. You don't go there. That's where you are. That's what you do. That's your purpose – to intercede.

- *Thank you, Father. Thank you for the new level of wisdom you're giving my sister, to call forth miracles for others.*

- *Go and walk in perfect health in Jesus' name.*

- *Father God, I thank you right now for my sister's healing.*

- *I call her cells to obedience.*

- *I call her body whole.*

- *I call forth her wellness.*

- *I call forth her strength.*

- *There is no weakness. There is no sickness. There is no ailing. There are no symptoms here in Jesus' name.*

- *We call her body restored.*

- *We call her spirit encouraged. We call forth her faith, enlarged.*

- *May her body remember my words and the words that Jesus loves her and heals her by His blood. That's the virtue in Jesus' name.*

- *May these frequencies remain in her body to bring forth those 31 frequencies we know this body needs.*

- *We call her body well and healed in Jesus' name.*

Prayer for an Intercessor 2

You are not healed for yourself. You are healed as a witness, as a testimony, to be the challenge to that sick and dying world so they too can walk and live in deliverance and healing. You will find those you will lay hands on and cause to be healed.

- *May the virtue of Christ go with you.*
- *May the virtue of healing be sustained in you in Jesus' name.*

Thank you Father for my sister's confidence. You have a radiance of confidence.

- *Father God, as you put faces before her, even in the night, of people she knows who are sick, who are diseased, who are spiritually sick, divorced, other problems, may my sister connect by her faith to your authority to call forth healing, not only for herself but for those around her, for loved ones, neighbors, friends, people at a distance and people far away.*

The Lord will give you that fresh prayer list. It will come fresh, and when you see those faces, you will pray for them. You are connected to them as you already know.

Prayer for Joints

- *I'm going to ask that His authority flow from the top of your body, through your mind, your spirit, your brain and your nervous system, down through your skeleton, down through your muscles, and down through your organs.*

- *Joints, you are made new by the authority of the designer. The designer's warrantee said that he could be healed in Jesus' name so we call forth his healing.*

- *We call forth his deliverance, that he can do his assignment without any pain and without any limitation.*

- *We call him healed in Jesus' name.*

- *Now, Father, we ask you to take away the symptoms of the memory of pain and of sickness. May he not have any pain.*

- *May the symptoms be removed because the bones are being restored.*

There have been those who have had an arm wounded in a war, or in a terrible accident, and they have removed the arm or the leg or limb. They have amputated it, and that victim feels pain of a missing limb the rest of their lives. That phenomenon is called **phantom pain**.

Doctors will verify it is a very real problem. When you are healed of a disease, healed, as in Jesus healing you or a doctor does a treatment giving you medication, and you are healed, your body can remember the symptoms. The symptoms can cause new problems for the body even though the disease has been healed. The body has phantom memory.

Why am I saying that? I'm saying that so that when you are prayed for, and you are blessed, you can be healed. I'm standing here as a testimony of healing. When you are healed, you pray with more authority. The person praying should remember to just dismiss the memory of the symptoms. I don't hear that prayed for very often, but when I pray for someone, **I dismiss the memory of the symptoms.**

As you move your legs and give them some motion, the authority of God is going to flow through these bones.

- *I dismiss doubt.*
- *I dismiss fear.*
- *He is healed in Jesus' name.*
- *Father, give him the confidence.*
- *Give him the evidence.*
- *May he wake with no pain.*
- *May he be able to run with no limits.*

He will honor you, Lord. He's going to serve the Lord. He's going to live for you. He's going to use this body for an assignment that requires it to be perfect.

- *We call forth his health and healing in Jesus' name. Amen and Amen and Amen. God bless you.*
- *Father God, we speak your energy into this neck. We speak your virtue, not mine Lord. My touch can't do it but your touch can, Lord.*

- *By the authority of Jesus Christ, I call his neck restored in Jesus' name. Restore.*

- *Body, be corrected. Respond to Jesus.*

Prayer for Joy

My sister, we've been praying for other bodies. What I prayed for other bodies, I pray the same thing for your body. God knows the difficulty. If there is a healing need, He is going to make your body whole. He is going to do it. It's not my authority. It's not my power, but it is my words. Church, it is your words. Careful with your words.

- *I declare in the name of Jesus, this body is healed.*

- *I declare that sickness has no place here.*

- *I declare that any fear she has had about some symptom or some pain or something that has been said is removed.*

- *The symptoms are gone. The sickness is healed.*

- *Your heart and your spirit are set free. Thank you. Thank you, Father. Bless her, Father.*

- *Heal her and restore her joy.*

- *I speak a happiness into you.*

I wouldn't be surprised if you break out laughing at new times. When there isn't anything funny to laugh about, you will have a spirit of joy come on you.

- *I call forth restoration of your joy in Jesus' name.*

- *Thank you, Father, for what you're doing right now inside of her.*

78

- *Thank you for what you're doing as she gets home tonight when she rests.*

- *When she lays down, may your presence rise strong within her.*

- *Close in on her in Jesus' name.*

I thank you for her.

Prayer for Liver

God can make all things perfect. You don't stand alone today. You stand in His presence, and He has diagnosed your body. We are going to the Designer who designed your purpose, who designed your assignment. He is going to give you strength.

- *Liver, you are obedient to the design of God.*
- *Blood pressure, you are obedient.*
- *Heal, Father.*

I know what it is to have blood pressure that can change in seconds. Thank you, Father, for changing my blood pressure, my heart, and my organs. I claim that for my sister. What you did for me is available for others because you are not a respecter of persons. You'll do it for her and everyone else in this line in Jesus' name.

- *So I declare you are healed, and I thank God for your healing.*

Say with your voice,

- *Thank you, Jesus, for healing my liver.*
- *Thank you, Jesus, for healing my body.*
- *All the toxic elements are gone in Jesus' name.*

Thank you. God bless you. Continue to rejoice. Continue to rejoice.

Prayer for Lung Cancer

You're about to be touched.

You say, "David, you say that very confidently."

If He can give me a new heart, there's nothing in your body He cannot fix. You can get new lungs right now. The symptoms can go away.

- *Father God, you know my sister. She needs new lungs to praise you and live for you.*

- *Father God, you caused this body to be.*

- *So Father God, I say in Jesus' name, there is nothing too big or too hard for my God. His blood was shed and will change even my sister's lungs.*

- *So we call her healed in Jesus' name.*

- *May your healing virtue go through her and may she know it.*

- *May she walk with newness of breath and newness of life.*

- *Change the cells.*

- *Change the DNA.*

- *Cancer, you're dismissed. Cancer you're gone in Jesus' name.*

Now, Father God, we worship you. We thank you. You are our Creator. You are our Savior. You are our healer. That blood we talked about was shed for my sister. So we thank you for that, and we know it has been applied in Jesus' name.

Prayer for Neck

- *I call this neck healed.*
- *Neck, you have no right to have pain and no reason to have pain.*
- *The virtue of Jesus Christ flows through this body.*
- *I declare this body whole, healed in Jesus' name.*

Now you have to observe yourself healed. You have to believe yourself healed, and He will cause it to be.

Prayer for Neighbor

You have the authority. You can do what I do. You can say what I say. Yes, Satan is bound up. You can say, **Satan has been found, and you can keep him bound!**

If he comes back, you can dismiss him. You can say,

- *You're gone in Jesus' name.*

He cannot be where Jesus' name has dismissed him. We don't have to wrestle with neighbors. Paul said we wrestle not with flesh and blood. We come against principalities. (Ephesians 6:12)

- *Father God, dismiss this man from that house.*
- *Remove him to a place where he won't cause problems for my sister.*
- *We have that right, that evil can be dismissed, and altered, and changed, and out of there.*
- *May someone become a minister to him.*
- *May my sister not have to wrestle or argue or even talk to him, except to say Jesus loves him.*

Believe he is blessed, then split. Don't argue with him. Don't carry on a big conversation with him. She doesn't need to hear his thoughts. He has nothing you want to hear except that he wants Jesus. You know how to pray.

- *Father, we call him delivered.*
- *We call him moved immediately in Jesus' name.*

I have been where there were businesses with employees and opposition from competition in the physical realm. I prayed to fix it, and someone's life changed.

Pray to "fix" someone
and see their life change

God is going to honor your righteousness, your prayer, and your faith. All the rest of it is Satan messing with you, and that is over in Jesus' name.

Prayer for Nerves

Thank you, Father, for my sister, for her skills, for her training and every experience. Father God, she has seen life and death.

- *I call forth life in her.*
- *I call forth from that invisible world completeness in her life as she walks in perfect health and energy.*
- *Her mind is clear. Touch her mind.*
- *Touch every neuron, every cell.*
- *Touch every connector.*
- *Touch every synapse.*
- *May she understand the elasticity.*
- *Her mind is altered by her beliefs and by her intent. Give her that revelation.*
- *May she know how to pray not only for her body, but for others' bodies.*
- *Father, we pray that my sister is healed, that she walks in health, that she walks in wellness.*
- *She walks in a place of blessing, with protection around her. Wherever she goes she is protected.*
- *She is a kingdom builder.*
- *May angelic hosts come upon her.*
- *May she walk in perfect health.*
- *No limits.*

- *No disease.*
- *Her assignment is being completed in Jesus' name.*

Prayer for Respiratory Problem 1

You don't need a respiratory problem with the flu. That's an easy one for Jesus. He can just dry you out right now. He can fix that.

- *Father God, you know what she has asked for.*

- *We declare that she is healed.*

- *And any other difficulties, Father, we call them healed.*

- *Father, we pray that this inconvenience is over with.*

- *Delivered, set free and healed, dried out, in Jesus' name.*

- *Father, may she know that this healing has happened.*

- *And may it be the stepping stone to greater healings to bring even more healings for others.*

- *Thank you for her faith.*

Thank you for this time of healing, in Jesus' name. Amen and Amen.

Prayer for Respiratory Problem 2

You didn't tell us anything God doesn't already know. He knows all of this. He knows what's wrong with the ears. He knows what's wrong with the eyes. He knows what's wrong with the breathing and the heart.

- *I speak to stress and I dismiss it.*
- *I speak nervous disorder and I dismiss it.*
- *I speak to the eyes and the ears and the brain and the nervous system, the heart and circulation, the respiratory system and call them healed.*
- *I called him healed.*
- *I call him delivered.*
- *I call the symptoms dismissed, even the coughing. Symptoms dismissed.*
- *Clear lungs. Clear bronchial tubes. Clear breathing. Take a big deep breath. Breathe in and breathe out. Thank you Father.*
- *Touch my brother.*
- *Set him free.*
- *Heal him.*
- *Give him the strength of body that gives him courage for his assignment.*
- *May he live his life and know his assignment.*
- *May it become the most important thing in his life.*

- *I call forth his habits to change and his life to change so that he will live with the purpose of his habit of serving you.*

- *His assignment. The purpose of every habit in his life is his assignment to serve you.*

- *Make him a kingdom builder.*

- *May the body give him all the energy and the strength he needs.*

- *May there be no disappointment from his physical body. Make him strong.*

- *Make him strong.*

- *Loosen tense muscles.*

- *Loosen tense joints.*

- *Heal him, Father.*

I think it is going to happen over time, a short time, maybe through the night. As you lay your hand on your body, wherever you put your hand, you will find healing. Move it across your lungs, across your heart, up over your eyes, gently touch your ears. You will find healing virtue.

- *Father God, may these hands carry healing virtue to this body in Jesus' name.*

Keep rejoicing. Keep thanking him. If you have God music, play it. Fill your life; let your ears hear your God music.

- *As praise goes in his ears, even coming from a recording, Father God, bring healing through that music in Jesus' name.*

Prayer for Shoulder

We're going to pray that Jesus touch you right now. Church, agree with me. Those who are seated look this way. Agree with me. Let's keep the unity.

- *Father God I pray for my sister that what's wrong with this shoulder is healed. Father God you raise the dead. You brought back to life the dead. The lame could walk. The lepers were healed. The blind could see.*

- *I declare my sister's healing.*

- *May your virtue flow through her. May she sense your energy flowing through her body.*

- *Cells obey. Disobedient cells, you're dismissed. No more disobedience.*

- *DNA take charge to rebuild her body, rebuild her shoulder.*

- *Remove the pain and give her rest.*

- *Give her the joy of healing, in Jesus' name.*

- *I say, God bless you. As I lay hands on that shoulder and the arm, in Jesus' name, we call her healed.*

- *The memory of the symptoms are removed. Symptoms are gone.*

- *Restore her youth.*

- *Give her health in Jesus' name.*

- Make her a witness to her friends, even to her doctor, in Jesus' name.

Prayer for Stroke Victim

- *Father, for the stroke victim, restore.*
- *Father, I know what it is to be a stroke victim, with the difficulties.*
- *So Father we call forth the restoration you gave to me to give to this person. Go up on them now.*
- *Rise strong within them.*
- *Deliver them neurologically.*
- *Give their body the right chemicals and oxygen.*
- *Restore their brain, Father, with the plasticity that it needs.*
- *We speak into it for correction.*
- *The fact that we're at a distance is not a problem with you, Lord.*
- *You're at all points across our trajectory.*
- *That includes the mind and the cells within that mind.*
- *We call the mind to obedience.*
- *We call it healed and delivered.*
- *We call our faith her faith, by proxy in Jesus' name.*
- *Thank you for my brother, Lord.*

- *Now, Father, as he prays for others, we stay in unity with him. I stand with unity to his faith and to his desire.*

- *So Father, may we stay connected even though I don't know what he's praying for.*

- *Help me to pray for him and his desire, and that will keep us connected, in Jesus' name.*

Thank you, Father. Amen. Isn't God good? And we cannot be disconnected. God bless you.

Prayer for Touching Doorknobs

When you touch the doorknob, say,

- *I bless this place.*
- *Evil is dismissed, in Jesus' name.*
- *Leave blessings wherever you go.*

Prayer for Work in Healing Rooms

Father God, give her an insight and a revelation. For anyone else, Father, who goes to the healing rooms, give them a revelation, a fresh revelation of who you are and what You want them to do.

- *May they hear Your voice and Your words to call forth deliverance for protection, to call forth deliverance from Satan.*

- *Give her wisdom.*

- *Give her authority.*

- *Father, I imbue into her the authority for healing.*

- *May she receive the anointing for healing, even in a prayer room,*

- *Father, touch her mind.*

- *Touch her spirit.*

- *I speak a blood shield over her that protects her mind, that protects her heart.*

- *May she not be attached to the kingdoms of this world or the events of this world in any way that would prevent her from being an authority for healing.*

- *May she understand the process of healing.*

- *May she understand the love of healing, the heart to call forth healing.*

- I impart that to her, the anointing for healing, in Jesus' name.

Prayer over Pictures in Newspaper

When you see a newspaper with all the evil and stories and pictures, lay your hand on those pictures, and you're hooked up. You're going to say,

- *I call this person blessed.*
- *I defect Satan from this person.*
- *The enemy of this idea is dismissed.*
- *The leader of this wrong thought or this sin or this greed or this graft or this corruption is dismissed.*

When you lay hands on the newspaper, you are doing so at the newspaper office because you are hooked up spiritually from that intent of what you know, and you're seeing what God sees.

When you see a picture in the paper of a person messed up with sin, lay hands on that picture. Say to that picture,

- *I call this man redeemed in Jesus' name.*

The Simplicity of Prayer

Now, you've listened to me pray. Maybe you've learned something about the simplicity of prayer. The simplicity of prayer you hear from me becomes the authority for you to use. Go there!

You heard me talk about science, and talk about things I know to be true. I give you reliable words. Go there!

Pray for the sick. Go lay hands on the sick. You have no right to doubt God. You have no right to lose a God idea. Go there, particularly those who are healed because now you have the healing as your evidence.

I have a new heart to prove that God is the God I'm talking about. Do you understand? Go there! You're going there!